Be Happy, Little Penguin!

Tiziana Bendall-Brunello

Illustrated by John Bendall-Brunello

NEW BURLINGTON

"Yippee, there's a dance at the zoo!" said
Little Penguin. "Oh, I wish I could dance!"

"Hello! What dance are you doing?"
asked Little Penguin.

"We're doing the swing!" replied the monkeys.
"Look – move your arms like us!"

"Feel the rhythm and move!"
said the orang-utans.

"I love the swing!"
laughed Little Penguin.

And then he tried to step...

and he tried to wiggle...

and he tried to jiggle.

"Mmm, that's an interesting dance," said Monkey.

"But it's not quite the swing,
is it?" said Little Penguin sadly.
    "It's a good start," said Monkey.
"You have to keep practising!"

And Little Penguin wandered off.
"Oh, I wish I could dance," he said.

Just then he heard some lovely
music coming around the corner.

"That's beautiful!" said Little Penguin. "What dance is that?"

"It's ballet!" replied Flamingo. "Do you want to try?"

"Yes, please!" said Little Penguin.

"On your toes...

and jump...

and twirl!" called Flamingo, as she
did a beautiful pirouette in the air.

Little Penguin tried to do the same.

Oops!

Whee!

"How exciting – I'm doing ballet!"
shouted Little Penguin.

"Wow! Is that modern ballet?" shrieked
the flamingos together, all excited.

"It's not quite there yet, is it?" sighed Little Penguin. "But I will keep trying." And off he wandered.

Little Penguin was about to give up and go home. Then he spotted some dancing hippos.

"Would you like to join our line dance?" asked the hippos, moving across the floor.

"Yes please, I would!" replied Little
Penguin, tapping his feet to the music.

And there Little Penguin was...

whirling on his back...

spinning on his belly...

and kicking his
little feet in the air!

Little Penguin felt
very happy. He was
having so much fun!

But when Little Penguin looked up, the others had stopped dancing. Suddenly they started clapping and cheering.

"That's a **brilliant** dance!" screeched the monkeys.

"Fantastic!" hooted the flamingos.

"What an amazing dancer!" roared the hippos. "You're a STAR!"

"So what do you call your new dance?" asked Orang-utan.

"Umm..." thought Little Penguin. "I think I'll call it break dancing," he said, "because it breaks all the rules!"

Notes for parents and teachers

- Look at the front cover of the book. Ask the children to name the animal. Can the children guess how the animal feels?

- Talk to the children about different kinds of dances: swing, ballet, line dancing and break dancing. Show the children how to do these dances. Ask the children to do any other dances that they may know.

- It is important to emphasize that in order to be good at something, children (a) should not give up too easily, (b) need to keep practising until they are good at it, (c) need to be patient and (d) should not worry about other people laughing at them because they are not yet good at what they are doing.

- Ask the children how Little Penguin becomes a winner. Discuss the different stages he went through – from the beginning when he started to learn to dance until the end.

- Children should be encouraged to ask other people for help when they need it. For example, Little Penguin is not afraid of asking other animals to show him how to dance.

- At the end of the story, ask the children to describe how Little Penguin and all the other animals and birds feel, and why.

- Ask the children to draw pictures of themselves dancing. Encourage them to explain how they feel when they dance.

Consultant: Cecilia A. Essau
Professor of Developmental Psychopathology
Director of the Centre for Applied Research and
Assessment in Child and Adolescent Wellbeing,
Roehampton University, London
Editor: Jane Walker
Designer: Fiona Hajée

A NEW BURLINGTON BOOK
First published in hardback in the UK in 2011
by QED Publishing
Part of The Quarto Group,
The Old Brewery, 6 Blundell Street
London, N7 9BH

Copyright © QED Publishing 2011

ISBN 978 1 78493 894 9

A catalogue record for this book is available
from the British Library.

Printed and bound in China